Mum Never Did Learn to Knock

Cathy Hopkins

Mum Never Did Learn to Knock

With illustrations by
Louise Wright

Barrington Stoke

For my mum, with thanks for always being there

First published in 2015 in Great Britain by
Barrington Stoke Ltd
18 Walker Street, Edinburgh, EH3 7LP

www.barringtonstoke.co.uk

This story was first published in a different form in
Like Mother, Like Daughter (Kingfisher, 2006)

Text © 2006 Cathy Hopkins
Illustrations © 2015 Louise Wright

A CIP catalogue record for this book is available
from the British Library upon request

ISBN: 978-1-78112-495-6

Printed in China by Leo

Contents

Chapter 1

Talk

There was a hammering on the bathroom door.

"Emily, who are you talking to in there?" Dad called.

"Speak later, Mum," I whispered into my mobile phone. "Don't worry, I'm on the case. I'll find out what I can." Then I popped the phone back in its case.

I opened the bathroom door with my best innocent smile. "I'm not speaking to anyone," I told Dad. "Just cleaning my teeth."

Dad didn't look convinced. "I heard you," he insisted. "You were talking to your mother again, weren't you?"

"No."

"Well, you were talking to someone."

I waved my phone at him. "Lou. I was talking to Lou, that's all," I said. "Homework thingy. So, what's for supper?"

'Change the subject fast,' I thought, because Dad's face showed concern.

"Takeaway or takeaway?" I said. "I fancy pizza. Four cheese. OK?"

We've lived on takeaways since Mum left. I did try and cook at first, but I wasn't too good at it. All I can do is cheese on toast, and Dad can only do scrambled eggs like rubber. Yuck.

Dad put his hand on my arm. "Emily …
would you … would you like to talk to
someone?" he asked.

"Someone?" I echoed.

"A counsellor."

"Like who? Not Aunt Iz, puleese. She lives
in wacko land."

Aunt Iz is Dad's barmy younger sister and
she calls herself a new-age counsellor. All
kinds of people go to her for healing-shmealing,
and she consults the Tarot cards and stars for
them and advises them to drink herbs that
taste disgusting. So, Aunt Iz? No, ta. Mum and
I used to joke that she was a witch.

"No, no, I mean a proper counsellor," Dad
said. "There are people trained to help with
what's happened to us."

'So now he thinks I need help,' I thought. 'Just because I've stayed in touch with Mum. I wish he'd see her or talk to her at least. She's looking great now. Loads better than before she left. Dad's the one that needs to see a counsellor. He's the one who's bottled everything up and thrown himself into his work so that he doesn't have to think about what happened.'

"No thanks, Dad," I said. "I'm fine. And I'll ... I've stopped talking to her."

'Liar, liar, pants on fire,' I thought. But what else am I to do? I'm not having people thinking I'm bonkers just because I want to talk to my mum.

Dad looked at the floor and shifted from one foot to the other. "It's not just me, Em," he said. "Miss Doolie rang from the school last night. They're worried about you there, too. She said you've been acting strangely – and it seems that you saw your mother at school."

'Well, I'm not likely to turn her away,' I thought, 'not now that she needs me.'

"Miss Doolie has fixed a time for you to see the school counsellor," Dad said. "On Monday lunchtime."

"Oh Da-ad," I moaned. "Gimme a break. I told you I've stopped talking to her, so I don't see what the problem is. Look, no way do I need to see a counsellor. That's for saddos."

Dad pressed my shoulder. "Do it for me, kid. I know these past weeks have been tough on you."

Chapter 2

All Right

'It won't be so bad,' I told myself the following Monday as I set off to see the counsellor. 'I bet she's one of those old hippie types like Aunt Iz. All long flowing skirts and big ethnic beads. I'll just say what she wants to hear and she'll be eating out of my hand.'

Aunt Iz was a pushover as long as you promised to keep an open mind and let her wave a crystal or two over you.

As I waited in the corridor, Mark Riley and Andrew Darby walked past.

"All right, Potts?" Andrew called. "In to see the shrink, are you? What you done? Wet your bed? Gone potty? Hey that's good, Emily Potts has gone potty."

"Get lost, potato head," I replied with as much disdain as I could muster. "I'm here because they think they might transfer me to a school for gifted pupils. They're worried that my natural talent is being held back because I have to mix with bozos like you."

Mark cracked up. He fancies me, I know he does. He told Avril Jeffries in Year 9 and she told Lou, and Lou told me. And he's OK for a boy. Cute, with no spots. He laughs a lot too. I like that.

"You? Gifted? Yeah right," Andrew said. "I knew you needed help."

At that moment, my mobile bleeped and the boys moved off so I could answer. It was Mum.

"Hey, Emily, sorry I haven't been in touch since Saturday. I'm still trying to adjust, you know …"

"I've been sent to see a counsellor, Mum," I said. "Everyone thinks I'm losing the plot because of you, so I'm going to have to be careful about talking to you from now on. A lot of people don't understand."

"Funny, isn't it?" she said. "If anyone needs a counsellor at the moment, it's me. No one prepares you for this, and I really don't know what I'm supposed to do next. It was so easy with your father. He always knew what to do."

"So why haven't you tried talking to him?" I asked.

"Oh I have," she said. "Don't think I haven't tried, but he's so closed-off. He just blanks me. It's like I've become invisible to him."

"It's just his way of dealing with it," I told her. "You know how he likes to keep things in separate boxes. That was then, this is now. That kind of thing."

"I know, love," she said. "Thank God I still have you."

The door opened and the school secretary stuck her head out.

"You can go in now, Emily. Mrs Armstrong is waiting."

"Catch you later," I said to Mum as I got up and switched off my phone.

Chapter 3

Gloria

It was dingy inside the counsellor's room and it smelled musty, like no one had opened the windows in years. There was a battered coffee table and three chairs that looked like they'd come out of a skip – one orange, one brown and one flowery – and there was a large box of tissues on top of the table.

'People must do a lot of crying in here,' I thought as a tall lady with white hair got up to greet me.

"You must be Emily Potts," she said as she offered me her hand.

I nodded. I'd tell her my name but nothing else.

"Take a seat," she said, and she pointed at a chair.

I did as I was told and sat opposite her.

"I'm Mrs Armstrong," she said, "but you can call me Gloria."

She was nothing like I expected. She was wearing a smart navy blue suit with high heels. She looked more like a business lady than the sort of touchy-feely type that wants to heal the world.

"You the counsellor?" I asked.

She nodded. "I am. Is that OK?"

I shrugged. "I guess."

She looked down at a book of notes, then back up at me. "So Emily, let's get down to business," she said. "Now. Do you want to tell me a little about yourself?"

I didn't, but I thought I'd better make some kind of effort. Hmm. What to say to keep her off the Mum trail?

"Um. Usual," I said. "Five foot two at the last count, but still growing – I hope. Medium build. Wish I was taller, wish I was thinner. I like Art and English. Don't like the colour of my hair. Dad calls it chestnut, but I think it's boring and I'd like some highlights, but he won't let me. Dunno. Usual stuff."

Gloria didn't seem that interested, but she made a few notes in her book. Then she looked back up at me. "Yes. I can see what you look like, Emily. What I meant to ask is, what's been going on with you the last while?"

I shrugged again. "Nothing. Same old, same old."

Gloria didn't smile. "I see," she said and made another note in her book. "So ... why do you think you've been sent to see me?"

I shrugged. "Dunno."

"OK, so how do feel about seeing me?"

"Dunno," I said again. "OK, I suppose." There was silence from Gloria so I thought I'd better add something. "How do you feel about seeing me?" I asked.

"I feel good about seeing you," Gloria said in a gentle voice that made me feel like throwing up.

'Why do people feel they have to be quiet around me now and treat me with kid gloves?' I thought. 'It's not like what happened is a first for the world.'

"But I'm concerned," Gloria went on. "Your teachers have told me about your mother."

"Have they?" I asked.

"They have," Gloria said. Then there was another long silence.

"What about her?"

Gloria coughed and shifted in her seat. "That she … she died three weeks ago."

"Yeah," I said. "So?"

"Well, your teachers told me that you talk to her," Gloria said. "I know, there's nothing wrong with that. A lot of people in your situation do. But you do know that she's dead, don't you?"

Another looooong silence.

I wondered if I was supposed to pitch in. Or was she waiting for me to break down and cry – was that why she had the tissues?

It was Gloria who cracked and spoke first. "I wonder … how do you feel about that?" she asked. Her voice was so soft I could hardly hear her.

I felt like laughing. 'How do I feel about that?' I said in my head. 'Oh, over the moon, Gloria. It's great to see your mum fade away in front of you. Best time of my life. Not.'

"How do you think I feel?" I asked. I was careful not to say the other words that I was thinking. Like, "You dingbat."

"Are you aware you keep asking me questions, Emily?" Gloria asked.

"Are you aware that you keep asking me questions, Gloria?" I shot back.

I mean, asking if I knew Mum was dead and how did I feel about it. How stupid can you get?

Of course I know Mum's dead. I was at her funeral. OK, it didn't sink in right away, because before that she'd always been there, every day, since I was born. I know that's obvious, but not everybody in your life has been there all the time from the start.

Chapter 4

Gone

It didn't seem real when Mum died. It couldn't be true. Like she'd gone to the hospital for a few days and would walk back in the door at any moment.

At first, I took a leaf out of Dad's book – I kept myself busy, tried to cook a bit, cleaned the house, did the washing and stuff. Tried to shut out the size of it. It wasn't like Mum's death was unexpected. She'd been ill for almost a year and we'd had long chats about how it would be when she'd gone. She was so organised about it all. She even chose the music, flowers and readings for her funeral. She was like that, Mum. Mrs Efficient.

Then, on the fourth day, it hit me that she wasn't coming back this time.

I was in the downstairs loo and it still smelled of her perfume. She always kept a bottle of it down there. Ô de Lancôme it's called. Light. Lemony. I realised that the scent would fade as Mum had.

I sat on the loo and reached for a piece of toilet paper, only to find that the roll had finished. There wasn't any more in the cupboard under the sink where Mum kept it. It was then that it hit home. My mum had gone. There was no one to buy the loo rolls any more. There was no one to take care of me any more.

I sat there and sobbed my heart out. It felt like a dam had burst inside of me.

All the feelings I'd been holding back flooded out, and a thousand questions flooded out with them. The biggest one was, "Where had Mum gone?"

I realised that in all the chats we'd had about her dying and how I would cope after, she'd never said one word about where she would be going. I couldn't believe we hadn't discussed it. Mum always left a note stuck on the fridge door when she went anywhere, even out to the shops for ten minutes.

I went into the kitchen to double check. But no, there was nothing. Only a Santa magnet from last Christmas. I opened the back door and yelled with all my breath into the night sky, "WHERE ARE YOU? M–UM. WHERE HAVE YOU GONE?"

A curtain twitched next door and I heard a window open, so I whispered it again, "Where have you gone?"

I kept asking myself over and over again –
"Where do people go when they die?"

So when Gloria asked if I realised that Mum
was dead, the answer was, "Yes." Oh most
definitely yes.

Chapter 5

Space

Gloria was still staring at me. Maybe she was waiting for me to say something or break down in tears, but I'd had enough.

There was nothing Gloria could say or do to help me. But I knew one thing for sure and that was that I didn't want to be coming to counselling every week for the next month. I had to bluff my way out.

"So, this talking to your mother ..." Gloria started.

"Listen, Mrs Arm ... Gloria," I said. "Yes, I do talk to Mum. It makes me feel better, like she can hear me somewhere, wherever she is. Like she's not really gone. I'm not mad or disturbed or anything. I'm fine, honest. I know she's dead."

Gloria looked at me kindly. "It must have been very hard for you," she said.

I nodded. "Yeah."

I wanted out of there. I wanted to hang out with Mark. After Assembly this morning, he'd asked what I was doing at lunchtime and even hinted that we could walk home together.

"But I'm OK," I told Gloria. "I've got my dad. And Mum told me she'd be watching over me and I could always talk to her. That's why I do it. I'm not loony petoony or anything. I'll be OK. I'm coping."

Gloria nodded and made a few notes on her pad.

I think I had convinced her that I wasn't out of my mind. She was just getting ready to round up our session, when Mum came in through the door. And I mean right through the door. Cool, that.

"All right, love?" she asked as she hovered behind Gloria.

I nodded and signalled for her to be quiet. Not that Gloria would see or hear her. Seems like it's only me that does that, but I didn't want to react or anything. I didn't want Gloria to clock that I wasn't just talking to Mum. I could see her. If Gloria thought that, then she'd think I was unhinged and I'd have to come back to counselling another time.

"I was just thinking," Mum said, as Gloria put her notebook into her bag. "Could you ask her if she knows where I'm supposed to go?"

"Um, Gloria, just one more thing," I said as Gloria got up.

Gloria smiled and sat down again. "Yes, Emily?"

"Er, where do people go when they die? I mean, where will Mum be? What happens when you die?"

Gloria went pale. "Er, well ... that's a big question."

"I know," I said. "Do you have the answer?"

Gloria looked at her watch. "I'm afraid we're out of time, Emily. Um. So many big questions in life – let me get back to you on that."

Mum stood next to me and we both watched Gloria, hoping that she was going to say something.

After a while, Mum shook her head. "I don't think she knows, love."

"Neither do I," I said.

"Pardon?" said Gloria.

"Oh. Nothing. I was just thinking, neither do I know where they go. Can I leave now?"

Gloria nodded. "Unless there's anything else."

I couldn't resist. "Just one more question, if you don't mind."

Gloria was beginning to look worried now. "Go ahead," she said.

"What's after space?" I asked.

Mum burst out laughing, because it was the question I used to drive her mad with when I was in junior school.

Gloria looked like she couldn't wait to get out of the room.

"My, but you're a curious child," she said. "Er. Can I get back to you on that as well?"

"Sure," I said. "Take all the time you need."

Gloria got up and rushed out of the room.

"Seems nobody knows," Mum said when she'd gone.

"Seems like," I said. "Sorry, Mum, but I told you – I'll do my best to find out."

Chapter 6

The Afterlife

After the meeting with Gloria, Mum hung around for the rest of the afternoon. It was a blast. She even peeked at Mr Parker's notes, then gave me all the answers for my History test. First time ever that I got an A.

After school, Mum didn't seem to be in a hurry to be off anywhere, and who could blame her – she didn't know where to go. She said she needed to be around someone she knew, and no way was she hanging out at the churchyard where she was buried.

"There are dead people in there," she said, then we both cracked up laughing.

It was brilliant having her around, and we joked about the fact that we spent more time together now she was dead than when she was alive. And it was easy to talk to her without anyone seeing, because I could get my phone out and pretend I was talking to someone on the other end.

I did try and tell my best mate Lou, but she didn't want to know. I think she's gone into the "Emily has lost the plot" camp, no matter how much I tell her that it's cool. She's terrified of ghosts.

"Mum says ghosts aren't scary," I told Lou. "They're the same as normal people."

"Duh, yeah, only one small difference," Lou said. "Like, they're dead."

She wasn't having any of it. It's because she watches so many horror films, so she thinks that ghosts are all scary. I know different now.

Mum said that just because you die, you don't have a personality change. She says it's fear of the unknown that scares people.

'Scares ghosts too,' I thought, but she's right about it being the unknown. It's weird. Death happens to everyone, and yet no one wants to talk about it, and no one really seems to know what happens.

Not that I wasn't scared when Mum first showed up. I was terrified.

I was in the bath, the night after I'd been shouting my lungs out in the back garden, and all of a sudden she floated out of the airing cupboard. Just like that. Dressed how she used to be in real life, in her old blue tracksuit and

trainers. My first reaction was to scream and close my eyes to make her go away. But when I opened them, there she was standing at the side of the bath.

We got talking, and that's when the trouble started and people began to think that I was disturbed and hadn't accepted Mum's death. Of course it wasn't that. I knew she was dead and wasn't coming back as she was before. But she was there in another form, no doubt about that, and she needed my help.

Sadly, our research into the afterlife only seemed to confuse things. There was loads of stuff out there – sites on the internet, books and magazines from the wonderful to the weird. Priests, gurus, philosophers, mystics, rabbis, all with their tuppence worth.

"What we need," Mum said, "is a sort of guide book. An A–Z of the afterlife, sort of thing."

"Probably have it in WH Smith's," I joked. "They sell maps. If not, we could always go back to the internet and type 'afterlife maps' into Google."

But we found nothing useful anywhere – zilch. I didn't care. It was great having Mum around.

Chapter 7

Mark Riley

One night after school, Mark was waiting for me by the bus stop.

"All right, Potts?" he said.

"Yeah. You?"

"Yeah."

'Hmm. So far a great conversation – not,' I thought, and I decided to take the plunge.

"Hey, Riley. You believe in ghosts?" I asked.

"I would if I saw one," he said, "but I haven't, so I can't say."

"But you don't not believe?" I said.

He looked at me. "No. Who knows? Why? You seen one?"

I looked at the ground. "Yeah. My mum."

"Get out of here," he said. "When?"

"All the time. She's always popping up."

"She all green and slimy?" He grinned.

I sighed. Another person who didn't take me seriously. "No," I said. "She looks like Mum. But see-through. And she smells different. Not like her old perfume any more. Her smell always arrives a moment before she does. It's divine, like a garden of roses in summer."

Mark looked a bit shifty. "Way to go, Potts," he said. "She around now?"

"No, but she will be later – that is, if she's not gone to see a movie."

Mark looked at me as if I was mad. I guess it did sound strange. Not your usual conversation with a boy you fancy. But then he smiled. "Why not?" he said. "Yeah. Cool."

"So you don't think I'm mad?"

Mark shook his head. "No," he said. "I've often wondered where people go when they die. My dog Petra died last year. It was awful. I mean, I know she was only a dog but she was like my best mate. I'd had her all my life. She always slept on the end of my bed. And then she wasn't there any more. I read everything I could about what happens next. Read up a lot about ghosts."

"So why do they stay around?" I asked. "I've been checking it out on the net, but everyone says different stuff."

"It seems," Mark said, "ghosts hang around for two reasons. One, they died in a sudden way and they're in shock, like they haven't adjusted to the fact they're dead yet –"

"That's not Mum," I broke in. "She knew she was dying for about a year."

"And two, unfinished business," Mark went on.

"Like what?" I asked.

"Dunno," Mark said. "Left the oven on. Something not said or done. Something to clear up with someone still down here. Feeling they still have to look after someone they've left behind. So why do you reckon your mum's still around?"

I shrugged, but I had begun to have an inkling.

Chapter 8

In the Bath

"What happened when you left your body?" I asked Mum later that evening, when she turned up in my bedroom.

"Ooh, it was lovely," she said. "I'd been drifting up a tunnel and then floated out at the end into a sea of white light. I felt surrounded by love and warmth. It felt like going home. I can't ever remember feeling so at peace. Then, all of a sudden, I had this terrible feeling that I'd forgotten something. Before I knew it, I felt myself being tugged back to Earth, and I found myself coming through the bathroom wall, and there you were. In the buff, in the bath."

"I know. You never did learn to knock," I said.

Mum grinned. "I would have if I could," she said, and she put her hand through the wall to prove her point.

"I ... I think I know why you came back," I said. "It was me. I cried out for you. It was when I realised that you'd gone. I felt such a massive sense of being alone. I was devastated. I think I brought you back. I was shouting out, 'Where are you?' because you'd forgotten to tell me where you were going. And I missed you and I wanted you back. I ... I didn't know at the time what would happen."

Mum tried to put her arm round me, but it kept going through me, so she held it a short way away, as if she was giving me a hug.

"I know, love," she said. "I'm sorry I couldn't let you know. Just ... I didn't know at the time. But it seemed that I was going somewhere very nice. Oh, I can't describe it, but it was a good place." Then her face clouded, which is an interesting look on someone who's see-through. Like a glass bowl that's steamed up. "But now I fear I might have missed the boat, or the ride, or whatever it was," she said.

"No. It can't be like that," I said. "It can't be like boarding a plane and if you miss your flight, you can't go. It can't be."

Mum shrugged. "Ah well. No doubt it will get sorted. So what are we doing tonight?"

"Ah …" I said.

Mark was coming over and I was hoping to see him on his own. I had a feeling that he wanted to kiss me but he didn't want to do it in front of Mum, and who could blame him? Dead or alive, having your mother watch your first kiss is uncool in anyone's book.

But I was in luck. I was saved from hurting Mum's feelings by someone ringing the doorbell downstairs.

"It's your Aunt Iz," Dad called up the stairs a few moments later.

"Maybe you'd better go," I said to Mum. She was looking out of the window, to try to get a glimpse of Dad's sister.

"No way," she said. "I wouldn't miss this for the world."

Chapter 9

Aunt Iz

We made our way downstairs. I walked, and Mum floated behind me like Mary Poppins. We found Aunt Iz in the kitchen. She had a dish of orange gloop with her, which she put on the table.

"A nice healthy lentil roast," she said, when she saw me looking. "I was worried you weren't eating right."

Mum pulled an "I'm-going-to-be-sick" face behind her. She never liked Aunt Iz's cooking either.

Over supper, we chatted about school and talked a little about Mum's death.

I had a hard time keeping a straight face as Mum was looning about the kitchen the whole time. She made mad faces and did her take-off of an Egyptian dancer in the air. That did it and I sprayed a mouthful of lentils everywhere and almost choked.

I think Aunt Iz thought my giggles were down to the fact I was seriously disturbed about Mum's passing. And so, when we'd cleared away the dishes, she came up with a plan to have a séance to try and contact Mum, so that she could let me know that she was OK. Aunt Iz roped Dad in too. At first he wasn't keen, because he's not into any of that heebie-jeebie stuff, as he calls it. But I talked him round and he agreed, if only to stop Aunt Iz fussing.

We lit candles, sat at the kitchen table and, after a few minutes, Aunt Iz started to sway about and roll her eyes.

I had to bite my cheeks to stop myself from laughing, and I could see Dad trying not to smile.

"I think … I'm … m-making contact," said Aunt Iz in a strange deep voice as Mum floated past and stuck a finger up her nose.

Of course, that set me off again and my shoulders started to shake with suppressed laughter. And then Dad got the giggles, even though he couldn't see what was really going on.

Mum was on a roll. She floated in and out the pantry door. Then she'd disappear altogether and just stick her leg through then back again, then her arm in and out, then at last her bum.

By this time, I was on the floor laughing, which soon snapped Aunt Iz out of her trance. And Dad had tears of laughter rolling down his cheeks at the sight of me as I tried to keep it together and failed.

"If neither of you are going to take me seriously, I'm leaving," Aunt Iz said. Then she stomped off and out of the front door in a huff.

After she'd gone, Dad and I looked at each other.

"More lentils, dear?" he sniggered.

"No, ta," I said, and we burst out laughing again.

Dad looked sad for a moment. "I think your mum would have enjoyed that," he said.

I put my hand over his. "Maybe she was watching us from wherever she is," I said.

"Maybe," Dad said softly.

Mum winked at me from behind him, then let her hand rest over his shoulder.

Chapter 10

Awkward Questions

For a few weeks, we had lots more fun. But the novelty of seeing Mum appear and disappear had begun to wear thin. I was seeing more and more of Mark. And that was the problem. I hadn't had a proper boyfriend before and Mum kept popping up at bad moments to ask awkward questions, like –

"How long have you known this boy?"

"Who is he? Where does he live? How old is he?"

"Has Dad met his parents?"

"Aren't you a little young for a proper boyfriend?"

"How serious are you about him?"

We could never get any time on our own. Mum followed us everywhere. Like when we went to see a movie, she turned up, sat behind us and coughed in my ear any time Mark put his arm around me.

When we were walking home through the park after school, Mum hid behind a tree. When we started holding hands, she leaped out with her Very Stern Face on. Because we were holding hands! And when we went on a picnic with some mates, she came along to that too and sat in between Mark and me like one of those old women that kept an eye on girls in the days when ladies wore bonnets. Course, no one could see her, but I think Mark thought it was odd that I didn't sit nearer to him. He'd been very understanding so far, but I still didn't want to tell him that my mum was stalking us

and watching and listening to everything we said and did. And I could have moved closer to him at the picnic, but no way was I going to sit on my mum's knee!

The lack of personal space at home had begun to get to me too, like how she came out of the bath plug when I was in the bath, or out of my knicker drawer when I was getting changed. Or woke me up early in the morning because she was bored and wanted someone to talk to or – in fact – to give me a lecture about boys. I felt bad about wanting some time to myself.

She was still my mum and I loved her, but I needed some space. I was so torn. There are lots of articles about how to deal with needy friends but none on how to deal with a clingy ghost – and the last thing I wanted to do was to hurt her feelings.

When we had time, Mark helped me do my research into the afterlife.

It seemed that a lot of people had had near-death experiences like Mum's. Perhaps their heart had stopped on the operating table, or they'd had a car accident or something, but later they'd come round to tell the tale. All of them seemed happy about dying since their near-death experience. In fact, some said they were looking forward to death when it happened for real, because they felt sure that there was somewhere wonderful to go to. Most of them said that they now believed that the body was nothing more than a shell that houses the real self.

And from what Mum had experienced when she first passed away, she had to agree. She had no worries about going "back up there" either.

Chapter 11

Roses

One night after school, Mark and I walked home through the park and we stopped at the big old elm tree by the railings.

He put his arms round me and I snuggled in.

"Is she around?" he asked.

I sniffed the air for her rose smell and shook my head.

He tilted my chin up and leaned in to kiss me. 'Get ready to pucker,' I thought, and I looked over his shoulder to make sure that there weren't any nosy neighbours around, ready to report back to Dad.

All of a sudden, the air filled with roses and Mum appeared on the other side of the railings.

I leaped back.

"What's up?" Mark asked. "Don't you want to?"

"No. Just ..."

"Ah," he said. "Your mum showed?"

I nodded. "Muuum ..." I began. I turned to Mark. "Can you give us a moment?"

He nodded and went off to look at the ducks in the pond a short way away.

"Look, Mum," I said, "you can't keep popping up everywhere. I do have my own life you know and ... it's a bit of a private moment here ..."

Mum had her Very Stern Face on. "I know what you were about to do, Emily Potts! You were going to kiss that boy."

I sighed. I felt bad about it, but I had to say something about her always following me. "Mum, you know I love you but … well, you wouldn't be with me all the time even if you were alive."

"You don't want me around, do you?" she asked.

"Yes, course I do but, OK … not all the time."

Mum looked sad for a moment. "I know, love. It's not as much fun as it was at the start, is it? Not for either of us. It's time. We've both got to move on."

A feeling of panic hit me. "No!" I said. "No. I didn't mean that –"

"It's time, Emily," she said again, and I noticed that she was beginning to look all shiny. She looked over at Mark down by the pond. "I just wanted to check you're all right," she said.

I followed her gaze. "I am. But that doesn't mean you have to go."

"I know, love," she said. "But I have to some time and ... well ... I ... I think I'm ready now and I think you are too."

Mum smiled at me and I felt her brush my cheek with her hand. Part of me wanted to yell, "Noooooo, not yet, just a little longer," but I knew she was right. It was time. If she stayed, there was no way forward for either of us. I had to let her go. It hurt inside, but I made myself smile back at her and I nodded.

And then she was gone. Just like that! I breathed in the last faint scent of roses and burst into tears. Mark was at my side in a flash and wrapped me in his arms.

"She's gone?" he asked.

I nodded and he held me until my tears had gone too.

Chapter 12

Sometimes

I never did see Mum again. But I still talk to her sometimes, and I'm sure she can hear, wherever she is.

I remember what she said about what happened when she first passed away, before I called her back. She said she had floated down a tunnel into a sea of light and that she felt surrounded by love and warmth and it felt like going home. So I don't feel worried about where she is any more, because I'm sure it's somewhere good.

And sometimes, just sometimes, like on my birthday, or days that for some reason I have the blues, I smell the scent of roses and know that she's never very far away.

Our books are tested
for children and young people by
children and young people.

Thanks to everyone who consulted on
a manuscript for their time and effort in
helping us to make our books better
for our readers.